He swung at the big curve and missed.

And then he swung and missed a fastball.

He was looking for the curve again. And he was right. This time he waited for it and hammered it hard.

The ball skipped in front of the shortstop and bounced off his chest. Jacob ran all out, hoping.

But the shortstop had time to chase the ball down and flip it to second for the force.

It was a close play, but Jacob watched the umpire and saw her right arm fly up, and heard her yell, *"Out!"*

So that was that.

Jacob had lost the game, all by himself.

Look for these books about the Angel Park All-Stars

#1 Making the Team
#2 Big Base Hit
#3 Winning Streak
#4 What a Catch!
#5 Rookie Star
#6 Pressure Play
#7 Line Drive
#8 Championship Game
#9 Superstar Team
#10 Stroke of Luck
#11 Safe at First
#12 Up to Bat
#13 Play-off
#14 All Together Now

ANGEL PARK All Stars

10

STROKE OF LUCK

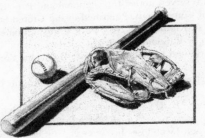

By Dean Hughes

Illustrated by Dennis Lyall

Bullseye Books · Alfred A. Knopf
New York

A BULLSEYE BOOK PUBLISHED BY ALFRED A. KNOPF, INC.
Copyright © 1991 by Dean Hughes
Cover art copyright © 1991 by Rick Ormond
Interior illustrations copyright © 1991 by Dennis Lyall
ANGEL PARK ALL-STARS characters copyright © 1989
by Alfred A. Knopf, Inc.
All rights reserved under International and Pan-American
Copyright Conventions. Published in the United States by
Alfred A. Knopf, Inc., New York, and simultaneously
in Canada by Random House of Canada Limited, Toronto.
Distributed by Random House, Inc., New York.

Library of Congress Cataloging-in-Publication Data
Hughes, Dean, 1943–
Stroke of luck / by Dean Hughes ; illustrated by Dennis Lyall.
p.   cm.—(Angel Park all-stars ; 10)
Summary: When Jacob loses his lucky charm, he's convinced he'll
never be able to bat, field, or throw again until he finds it.
ISBN 0-679-81537-6 (pbk.)—ISBN 0-679-91537-0 (lib. bdg.)
[1. Baseball—Fiction. 2. Luck—Fiction.] I. Lyall, Dennis,
ill. II. Title. III. Series: Hughes, Dean, 1943–   Angel Park
all-stars ; 10.
PZ7.H87312St   1991
[Fic]—dc20   90-53313

RL: 4.2
First Bullseye Books edition: April 1991
Manufactured in the United States of America
10 9 8 7 6 5 4 3 2 1

for David Ramsey

★ 1 ★

Hot Day

Jacob was nervous as he walked to the batter's box. He slid his hand into his pocket and gripped his lucky coin.

The game was in the second inning, and there was no score so far. But the Dodgers had runners on first and second.

The Padres had improved a lot this year. A kid named Hugh Roberts had grown about six inches and had become a pitcher. The guy could really *steam* the ball.

Everyone called him Bad News.

A tall, skinny guy named Brenchley was now catching for the Padres. He wasn't as good as Cegielski, last year's catcher, but he thought he was the best ever.

As Jacob stepped into the box, Brenchley mumbled in his deep voice, "Bad News is wild today. You better stay loose."

Brenchley wasn't lying either.

Roberts hadn't given up a hit so far, and he had struck out Jonathan Swingle and Sterling Malone, two of the Dodgers' best hitters. But he had walked three—including the two on base now.

Jacob took a couple of warmup cuts, and he acted as though he hadn't heard Brenchley. But he gave ground on the first pitch.

"*Strike one!*" the umpire called.

Brenchley laughed. "What are you jumping back from, kid? Just wait until one gets away from him."

Jacob stepped out of the box. He used his bat to knock dirt from his shoes, and then, as usual, he pretended he was a radio announcer. But he spoke only to himself, very quietly. "This Bad News is a pretty fair pitcher, Hank, but he's up against Jacob Scott, one of the best hitters in the league."

"You got that right, Frank," he answered himself with a cowboy twang. "This kid ain't afraid of *nobody*."

"What did you say?" Brenchley was asking, but Jacob paid no attention. He slipped his fingers around the coin again, and then he stepped back to the plate.

This time Jacob held his ground and took a nice stroke. The bat connected—*cleanly*—and the ball shot past the third baseman on a line. It bounced and rolled all the way to the left field corner.

The fielder—a girl named Jorgensen—was very fast, but she had a long way to run.

Jenny Roper, the only girl on the Dodgers, stormed around third and scored easily.

Billy Bacon chugged past second and coasted into third. But Jorgensen's throw was wide and got away from the third baseman.

Billy scored, and the Dodgers were ahead 2 to 0.

Jacob held up at second. He stood on the bag and waved his fists to his friends Kenny Sandoval and Harlan Sloan. The three of them had been rookies together the year before, but now they were fourth graders and proud of it.

"Let's keep it going," Jacob yelled. And then he touched his coin again. Maybe the thing really *worked!*

It was an old coin minted in honor of the San Francisco world's fair. It wasn't worth much, but his grandpa had given it to him and said it was lucky. Grandpa had laughed when he said it, though, and Jacob hadn't taken it too seriously.

Now he was starting to wonder.

When Lian Jie lined a drive up the middle and Jacob scored, he wondered some more. This was some coin if it would help the Dodgers beat Bad News.

Things even got better in the bottom of the inning when Jacob went out to play right field. The Padres' lanky first baseman hit a looper that was dropping fast. Jacob charged hard, dove, and caught the ball just above the grass.

Suddenly he felt that he could do no wrong today.

And things were looking up for the Dodgers. Jonathan was pitching well, and he had a three-run lead to work with. The season had started slow, but now the Dodgers were playing the way they knew they could.

When the inning was over and Jacob trotted to the dugout, Coach Wilkens

stopped him. "Great catch, Jacob," he said. "But if that kind of ball gets by you, it could be big trouble. Never leave your feet unless you're *sure* you can get it. And always keep the ball in front of you."

Jacob nodded, but he thought the coach shouldn't worry so much.

Everyone in the dugout slapped hands with Jacob. Big Jonathan said, "Hey, Jacob, you're getting it done for us today. You've got more RBIs than . . ." But then he laughed and said, "Never mind."

Jacob knew what he meant. Jonathan loved to be the best at everything, and he liked to keep track of his stats. But the coach kept reminding him that baseball was a *team* sport, and Jonathan was trying to keep his head straight about that.

Or at least he said he was.

Jacob sat down on the bench next to Ben Riddle and Anthony Ruiz, this year's rookies. "Nice catch, Jacob," Anthony said. "I wish I could do that."

"You will," Jacob told him.

Anthony shook his head, as if to say "Fat chance."

"No, really, Anthony. I was so bad when

I first made the team. So was Harlan. But we just kept working hard, and we're getting better. We still practice almost every day."

"Could we practice with you?" Ben asked.

"Sure. Come over to the park after school. We're here almost every day."

Jacob felt sorry for Anthony and Ben. Anthony was chubby and slow—and sort of awkward—and Ben played as though he were afraid of the ball. Neither one had gotten a hit so far in the season.

Jacob knew that Coach Wilkens had seen something in these guys or he wouldn't have chosen them. But right now it was hard to see what that was. Maybe they had played better in practice, when they hadn't been up against so many older guys.

"Here, rub my lucky coin," Jacob told Ben and Anthony. "It's helped me today." He grinned, showing the split between his front teeth. He was a freckle-faced kid who smiled a lot.

Both guys took the coin and rubbed it.

"I wish it would work," Anthony said.

"It's going to take more than a lucky

charm for us to get hits off that Bad News guy," Ben said.

Jacob had to admit that was probably true. But he didn't say it.

Kenny Sandoval was up first. But he was not as lucky as Jacob had been.

He hit a hotshot grounder that almost took the shortstop's glove off. But the shortstop, a new kid named Palmer, stayed with it and threw Kenny out.

"That's all right, Kenny," Jacob shouted to him. "You hit the ball *hard.*"

"Yeah," Billy shouted to him, "I hope that kid doesn't like to suck his thumb; I think you broke it off."

But the Padres' fans were talking it up. They had come to Angel Park sure they could beat the Dodgers this year. So far, Jacob wasn't impressed.

When Jonathan smacked a solid single and Sterling walked, Jacob figured the Dodgers might even get some extra runs.

But it wasn't to be. Jenny flied out, and Eddie struck out.

The score was still 3 to 0 going into the bottom of the third.

And then, suddenly, the game turned upside down.

Jonathan walked the right fielder. Then Palmer knocked a drive into center for a single. Everything seemed all right when Jonathan got tough and struck out the next two batters.

But then Bad News Hugh came to bat. The guy could hit.

Someone on the Padres' bench yelled, "You'd better get ready for some *BAD NEWS*, Dodgers!"

The Padres' families were also making a lot of noise. One guy—probably Roberts's dad—kept bellowing, "Knock the cover off the ball, Hugh."

Roberts looked as if he thought he could do it too.

But Jonathan fired a fastball past him.

Jacob heard Billy's mitt *POP* all the way out in right field.

Jonathan got the ball back and powered another pitch the same way.

But this time power met power. Bad News connected.

The ball arched high and long over Jacob's

head. Jacob broke into a run, but the ball was carrying forever.

It landed well beyond the right field fence. And the game was all tied up.

★ 2 ★

Charmed

When the inning was over, Jonathan walked to the dugout and threw his glove against the fence.

Michael Wilkens, the coach's son and assistant coach, followed him into the dugout. "Jonathan," he said, "you didn't throw a bad pitch. He just hit it. That kid's a good athlete."

"He's got a *big mouth*," Jonathan said.

Michael smiled. "Yeah, well, there are a few of those around here."

Jonathan seemed to know what Michael meant. He was not exactly a quiet boy himself. He nodded, and then he even smiled a little.

"Come on, team," Jonathan yelled, "let's get some runs!"

Jacob was looking for his bat. And he was excited. He had a feeling he could get another hit off Roberts.

Harlan, batting for Billy, grounded out, so Jacob knew he would have to be the one to get things started.

But Bad News threw some real *heaters*.

Jacob rubbed his coin between pitches and waited for his chance. When the count reached 3 and 2, something had to happen.

Jacob swung a little late, but he got his bat on the ball. He dribbled a slow grounder to the right side.

The first baseman hurried forward, grabbed the ball, and spun. The second baseman was covering first.

The throw was close, but Jacob beat it.

And this time he *knew* he had lucked out.

"You call that a hit?" Bad News barked at him.

Jacob grinned at him. "Sure. That's what *I* call it." And then, under his breath, he added, "Well, Hank, Scott has it going today. Everything is working out for him."

But Jacob was having more luck than all the rest of the team together. Lian struck out—something he almost never did. And Henry White, one of the team's best hitters, hit a weak grounder.

Jacob was stranded at first.

In the bottom of the fourth the Padres' coach worked his substitutes into the lineup. Jonathan blew them away.

Then, in the top of the fifth, it looked as though the Dodgers might get something going when they sent up their power hitters: Kenny, Jonathan, and Sterling.

But all the Dodgers got were goose eggs. Kenny hit the ball hard again, but he flied out. Jonathan and Sterling both seemed too anxious. They swung at bad pitches and grounded out.

So the score was still tied, and now the coach was putting Ben in for Lian at second base. That could be trouble.

At least Coach Wilkens put Anthony in left field—and left Jacob in the game. Maybe, he thought, with Jonathan throwing so hard, the batters would swing late and hit the ball to right.

All Jacob knew for sure was that good things were going to happen to him. As he ran past Ben at second, he stopped and pulled out his lucky coin. "Hey, Ben, touch this," he said. "It's working!"

Ben smiled and rubbed his fingers across the coin. "You've got it made now," Jacob told him, and then he ran out to right field.

Whatever the coach's hunch had been, things worked out right—in right.

The first batter hit a screamer to right field, and Jacob dropped back quickly and caught it. Anthony might have had trouble with a ball like that.

But the next batter rolled a grounder toward Ben, and Jacob held his breath.

Ben actually moved toward the ball, the way he had been taught.

The ball took a nice big hop just as Ben stuck out his glove.

The ball *STUCK!!!*

For a moment Ben seemed to hesitate, as though he had forgotten what to do. But then he dug the ball out of his glove and made the short throw to first—in plenty of time.

Ben had helped make a put-out.

The whole team cheered for him, and somewhere in the stands Jacob heard Ben's mother yell, "Way to go, son!"

Ben turned around and gave Jacob a big thumbs-up.

Jacob was just happy to share the luck.

When Jonathan struck out the next batter, Jacob charged back to the dugout. He checked the lineup. He would be the fourth batter, so someone had to get on. He wanted to bat.

It was the sixth inning, and the score was still tied. Jacob wanted to use his good luck to win this game somehow.

Jenny was up first, and Anthony was on deck.

"Hey, Anthony, come here," Jacob yelled.

Anthony was kneeling in the on-deck area, but he got up and trudged to the dugout. Jacob held out his good-luck coin and said, "Rub this. Ben did, and he made his first good play."

Anthony's slow smile appeared. He rubbed one finger over the coin and nodded.

But when Bad News struck out Jenny, Anthony glanced back at Jacob. He looked scared to death.

He walked slowly to the batter's box and stood with his bat barely off his shoulder.

"Come on, Anthony!" Jacob yelled. "Luck is with you this time. You're going to do it."

The first pitch slammed past Anthony, and he didn't move.

"Strike!"

"Hey, fat boy," Brenchley said. Jacob couldn't hear the rest. What he did hear was the umpire telling Brenchley to lay off that stuff.

The next pitch was another strike, and Anthony still didn't move.

And then he *had* to move. The ball was right at him. He cringed and dropped to the ground, but the ball glanced off his helmet.

Coach Wilkens ran toward him, but Anthony got up and said he was okay.

He picked up his bat as though he were ready to go back to the plate. The ump said, "You got hit. Take your base."

Jacob saw Anthony smile just a little. Then

he gave the bat a polite toss and jogged slowly to first.

Maybe it was a strange way to get lucky, but at least he was on base. Still, Jacob knew how slow Anthony was. He would probably have to be on third to have a chance to score.

But no such luck. Harlan popped up.

Jacob would just have to keep things going somehow.

Brenchley's mouth was going when Jacob stepped up to the plate. "No little kid is going to get three hits off Bad News in one day," he said.

Jacob ignored all that and got ready. And then he remembered something.

"Time-out," he called. And he stepped out of the box. He acted as though he had to wipe sweat from his eyes. Then he tucked his fingers into his pocket and got a quick touch from the good-luck coin.

He stepped back in, and he watched that first pitch spin toward him. His mind registered "curve . . . wait," and then he felt the wood of the bat connect with that perfect . . . *CRACK!!!*

The ball shot into the left-center gap and rolled between the outfielders.

Jacob ran hard and was rounding first and going all out before he realized he had almost caught up with Anthony.

The two of them rolled around second.

And then Jacob jammed on the brakes. He would have to hold at second and let Anthony stop at third.

But the coach was waving Anthony on. Jacob shot a glance to the outfield and saw that the center fielder was finally picking up the ball, near the fence.

Anthony was thundering past third, but he was huffing and puffing and getting slower all the time.

Jacob took off again for third. He watched the cutoff man.

The shortstop took the throw. He spun and hurled the ball home. Brenchley was waiting, set solid, blocking the plate.

Anthony was pounding home on a collision course.

Both arrived at the same time.

Anthony and the ball.

Brenchley took the throw and turned just

as Anthony took a late, clumsy slide. He crashed over Brenchley like a falling wall.

When all the arms and legs were untangled, Anthony rolled off Brenchley and touched home plate.

"Safe!" the umpire wailed.

And then Jacob saw the ball. It was lying in the dirt where Brenchley had dropped it.

The Dodgers went nuts.

★ 3 ★

The Search

The Dodgers congratulated Anthony—
mostly for his rhino-style "slide"—and they
pounded Jacob's back until he thought he
would be bruised.

But he didn't mind. This had been *some*
day.

Of course, the game wasn't over. Jacob
ended up stranded on third, and the
Dodgers were only one run ahead going into
the bottom of the sixth.

But Jonathan was ready. He got Jorgensen
on an easy come-back grounder. Then he
finally got Roberts out on a little fly to Kenny
in short left field.

But the icing on the cake was ending the

game by striking out Brenchley. The guy still looked a little dazed—after the great collision—and he had nothing at all to say.

Once the Dodgers had slapped hands with the Padres, they settled down for the coach's usual after-game talk.

"Some of the younger guys really played a big part in this game," he said. "Jacob had a great day, and our rookies came through when we needed them. I liked the spirit out there today. You were all pulling for each other."

He looked right at Jonathan, and Jacob saw Jonathan nod. Something good was starting to happen there.

The players had their usual drinks, and lots of parents came around to congratulate them. Everyone told Jonathan what a great game he pitched, but Jacob got the most attention.

Harlan said, in a loud voice, "Jacob was three for three, with two RBIs. How's that for a day?"

"Yeah, but I gotta admit," Jacob said, "I had some extra help. I had my lucky coin with me." He reached in his pocket to pull it out.

But nothing was there.

He tried again. He shoved his hand deeper, felt all around.

"Oh, my gosh!" he said.

"What's the matter?" Kenny asked him.

"I lost it! My good-luck coin!"

Jacob spent almost an hour looking for the coin, and he had plenty of help. Kenny and Harlan stayed, and so did Anthony and Ben.

At first Jacob thought he must have lost it when he slid into third, so he and the other boys looked all around the base and in the grass close by. They even got down and raked their fingers through the dirt.

Then he thought he might have pulled it out accidentally when he had touched it just before he batted.

Same search. Same result.

Then he thought maybe it had worked its way out while he was running. That meant checking all around the base paths.

Still nothing.

Finally he decided it had to be in right field. But this meant searching in the grass.

The boys took a lot of time, walking and watching for something shiny.

But they still found nothing.

And so they finally gave up and walked home together. But Jacob felt rotten. He didn't like to think a silly good-luck piece could make that much difference—but he had been three for three.

"Look at it this way," Kenny told him. "Maybe it wasn't luck. Maybe you just played well. That's a better way to think about it anyway."

"That's how you think of everything, Kenny. But don't forget that time you got jinxed last year, and *I* figured out how to change your luck."

"No way," Kenny told him. "I had a slump, and then I got out of it. That's all."

"You'll never make it to the major leagues thinking that way," Jacob told him.

All the boys laughed, but Jacob didn't. They had reached his house, and they all stopped out in front.

"Laugh all you want," he told them. "But major-leaguers almost all use tricks to get good luck. I've read about it in books."

One thing was sure: Jacob had read more about baseball than *anyone*.

Jacob saw that he had them thinking. "How come so many great players have lucky shirts and socks, and stuff like that?"

"Not all of them do," Kenny said. "Some of the best players don't believe in stuff like that."

Jacob gave up. He was mad that Kenny wouldn't try to understand. He wasn't so sure the coin helped either. But what did it hurt to hope so?

"I'll see you guys," Jacob said softly, and he headed up his front walk.

Kenny said to Jacob's back, "I just thought you *played* well. Play the same way next time."

That was easy for Kenny to say. Kenny was so good he didn't need luck on his side. But Jacob told himself that he needed all the help he could get.

That night Kenny called Jacob and tried again to convince him that the coin hadn't made any difference.

But Jacob wouldn't listen. He had a plan. His uncle owned a metal detector. And

his cousin had agreed to use it to try to find the coin.

Kenny told him he was going to practice at the park the next day anyway, and he wouldn't mind helping him look.

But he still thought it was a waste of time.

All the same, on Thursday Jacob got Harlan and Ben and Anthony to help—along with Kenny and his cousin—and they went over the whole diamond and all of right field.

Inch by inch.

But still no luck.

Kenny kept trying to tease the guys out of taking the whole thing so seriously.

But Ben was just as concerned as Jacob. He was down on his knees with a magnet. He kept pushing it slowly through the grass. He finally told Kenny to quit kidding around. "We've *got* to find it."

Ben was a quiet kid, and he didn't often give his opinions. Everyone seemed a little surprised.

"What's the big deal?" Harlan asked.

"Jacob let me touch it, and then that grounder came to me, and I made a good play."

"You've also been practicing a lot," Kenny said. "Maybe that had something to do with it."

"Maybe. Maybe not." Ben wore glasses, and he had a way of leaning his head down, as though he could see better when he looked through the top of the lenses. But that only made his shaggy black hair fall in his eyes. The truth was, he didn't look much like a ballplayer. He looked a lot more like a nerd.

"Ben," Kenny said, "the coin had nothing to do with it."

"I think it did," Ben said. He nodded and gave Jacob a look that said "I'm sticking with you, Jacob."

But Jacob thought he finally had the right idea. "Practice *and* luck. That's the combination a guy needs."

"I'll stick with practice. Luck evens out after a while," Kenny said.

But Anthony had obviously been thinking things over. He was ready with his opinion. At the moment he was checking something shiny he had spotted, but it turned out to be a candy wrapper.

He looked up at Kenny with those big,

soft eyes and said, "I didn't run any faster after I touched the coin, but that catcher dropped the ball. That was luck."

"Not really," Harlan said. "If you had slid the right way, you would have been out. It was *lack* of practice that paid off for you."

Harlan grinned.

"Yeah, well, that's luck, if you ask me," Jacob said. But he grinned too. "It's hard to know when to do the *wrong* thing at the *right* time."

The truth was, Jacob was getting a little nervous that the rookies were taking this thing even more seriously than he was. Jacob wanted to stay lucky, but he also wanted to believe that he was playing better all the time.

He told himself that practice really was more important, and that he'd better do some of that right now.

And yet . . . if he could just find that coin, he really would feel a lot better.

BOX SCORE, GAME 4

Angel Park Dodgers 4

	ab	r	h	rbi
Jie 2b	3	0	1	1
White 3b	3	0	0	0
Sandoval ss	2	0	0	0
Swingle p	3	0	1	0
Malone cf	2	0	0	0
Roper 1b	2	1	0	0
Boschi lf	2	0	0	0
Bacon c	0	1	0	0
Scott rf	3	1	3	2
Sloan c	2	0	0	0
Ruiz lf	0	1	0	0
Riddle 2b	1	0	0	0
ttl	23	4	5	3

Santa Rita Padres 3

	ab	r	h	rbi
Lundberg 2b	3	0	0	0
Jorgensen lf	3	0	0	0
Roberts p	3	1	2	3
Brenchley c	3	0	0	0
Durkin 1b	1	0	0	0
Blough 3b	1	0	0	0
Valenciano cf	1	0	0	0
Campbell rf	1	1	0	0
Palmer ss	2	1	1	0
Orosco 1b	1	0	0	0
Nakatani 3b	1	0	0	0
Rollins cf	1	0	0	0
	21	3	3	3

Dodgers 0 3 0 0 0 1—4
Padres 0 0 3 0 0 0—3

★ 4 ★

Giant Trouble

The boys didn't find the coin, but by Saturday morning Jacob had decided that Kenny was right. Lucky charms were silly. He had played well against the Padres. Why call it luck?

Sure, major-leaguers liked to fool around with lucky shirts and things, but they probably didn't take it all that seriously. He wished he hadn't made such a big deal out of the whole thing.

The *real* worry was the Giants. They hadn't lost a game. They had two good pitchers, and Dave Weight, their star hitter, was knocking the fences down. In fact, the whole team was hitting well.

Before the game Kenny was getting ready to pitch, and Jacob could see that he was nervous. "Hey, Kenny," Jacob said, "we can get these guys. I'm not going to worry about that coin."

Kenny nodded, and then he whistled a warmup pitch to Harlan. "These guys are tough," he told Jacob. "They lost Halliday and Crandall, but everyone else is back from last year."

"That's okay. We're playing better now too. We'll back you up on defense."

And Jacob soon made good his words. In the first inning Weight came to bat with a guy on first. He hit a bullet. But Jacob got a good jump and ran it down near the foul line.

If the ball had gotten past Jacob, it would have gone for extra bases. But now Kenny got the next batter to ground out, and the inning was over.

Back in the dugout Kenny told Jacob, "See, you don't need luck. You just need to play like that."

Jacob nodded. It was nice to think he didn't need charms—skill was enough.

"All right," Billy was shouting, "let's get it going now. Everybody hits. Let's tear down the 'House.'"

"House" Hausberg was pitching for the Giants. He was a huge guy, but he didn't throw all that hard. He just had better control than most Little League pitchers.

And he had the best curve ball in the league. He could get it over the plate, and he wasn't afraid to throw it with two strikes on the batter.

"Wait on his curve," Henry yelled to Lian.

Lian smiled and nodded. And then he took his stance. He had good, quick wrists and great bat control.

Hausberg came with his curve on the second pitch, and Lian stayed with it and poked it to the right side.

Base hit.

Henry tried to do the same. But he topped the ball and rolled it to the second baseman. The Giants took the force at second. Henry was on at first on the fielder's choice.

Kenny walked to the plate.

The Giants talked it up, but they weren't yelling any insults this year. The Giants had

a new coach, a slim young man. He was more like Coach Wilkens. He wanted his team to show some sportsmanship.

House came with a fastball and showed he could power one when he wanted to.

Kenny didn't pull the trigger and took a called strike.

Jacob could see that Kenny was upset with himself. He stepped out of the box for a couple of seconds and then got back in.

"Hey, Kenny," Jonathan yelled from the on-deck circle, "watch for the curve."

But Hausberg came with his heat again, and Kenny was ready. He met the ball— *bam!*—and laced it into center field.

The ball was hit so sharply that it got to the fielder quickly, and Henry had to stop at second.

Jonathan trotted to the batter's box. Jacob could see that he could hardly wait.

All the Dodgers were hollering their heads off now. They really wanted to get something going early against the Giants. This was a big game if they were going to have a chance for the first-half championship.

"This guy's no house," Billy was telling his teammates. "He's an outhouse. He stinks."

The Giant infielders were all up on their toes, waiting and yelling, "Hey, batta, batta, batta."

The fans were already into the game. Lots of people had come over from Blue Springs, but there were plenty there from Angel Park, and they all seemed to be yelling too. They knew this was the biggest game so far this year.

Jonathan took a fastball inside, and the noise quieted for a few seconds.

Then it started all over again.

And this time the big, sweeping curve was on its way.

Jonathan waited, waited, and then . . . *crash!*

He powered the ball into left field.

The ball carried high and long. Jacob couldn't tell if it would be . . .

And then it hit the top bar of the fence and bounced over.

Home run!

Suddenly the Dodgers had jumped on top, 3 to 0. Big House Hausberg didn't look tough at all to the Dodgers.

And luck seemed to be with them, coin or no coin.

All the players ran from the dugout and met the runners as they crossed the plate. Everyone slapped Jonathan's hand, and then they all ran back to the dugout together.

"Let's keep it going," Jonathan kept yelling. "Let's get some more runs *right now.* Let's blow the *House* down."

But that didn't happen.

Sterling Malone fouled off a couple and finally struck out. Jenny hit the ball, but she got under it and lifted an easy fly to right field.

Still, the Dodgers were in good shape. And things kept getting better. Jacob made another good catch in right, and the Giants went out in order in the second.

And then Jacob started off the bottom of the inning with a hard shot to left field. He was tempted to try for two, but he held at first, and it was just as well. Eddie Boschi, the skinny left fielder, struck out, but Billy hit a double into the right field corner, and Jacob scored all the way from first.

Then Henry drove home Billy with another hard-shot single.

The score was 5 to 0.

The Dodgers almost got two more when Kenny skied a long fly to center field. But he hit the ball to the deepest part of the park, and the fielder got back and made the catch.

All the same, when the Dodgers took the field in the top of the third, they were feeling that Hausberg was no problem and that Kenny was going to hold the Giant hitters anyway.

And all Jacob could think was that he had been stupid to worry so much about a so-called lucky coin.

But then the first Giant batter in the third inning swung off stride and chopped the ball into the ground. It took a high bounce on the infield. Henry grabbed for it and then hurried his throw.

The ball bounced in the dirt. Jenny made a good stop on it, but the runner was safe.

It was a lucky hit.

But Kenny wasn't bothered. He moved the ball in and out on the next batter and then struck him out on a high, hard fastball.

Nugent, the lead-off batter, did no better. He hit an easy grounder to Jonathan,

who flipped the ball to Lian, who covered second for the force. The Giants had two outs.

Things were still rolling along.

The Dodgers talked it up. Jacob could feel the confidence. The team was really coming together.

Then Sanchez, the shortstop, surprised everyone with a bunt. Henry charged it, but he had no chance. Sanchez was a flier.

That brought up big Dave Weight with two on and two out.

Kenny came with a fastball and then tried his change-up.

Weight guessed right. He waited on the pitch and poked it to the right side.

Jacob charged hard.

He knew he couldn't catch the ball in the air, but if he could cut it off quickly and make a hard throw home, the runner from second might not score.

But Jacob glanced at the runner and took his eye off the ball. It took a flat hop at that moment and skipped under his glove. By the time he reversed himself, got to the ball, and threw it back to the infield, two runs had scored and Weight was on second.

Then Glenn hit a seeing-eye grounder up the middle and Weight scored.

Suddenly the score was 5 to 3.

Jacob kicked at the grass.

He had messed up. But he had gotten a bad break too—the way the ball had bounced.

His fingers had already sneaked into his pocket for a touch of the coin before he remembered that it wasn't there.

No matter what he had said before, he wished he had it back.

★ 5 ★

Second Chance

"I'm sorry I made that error," Jacob told Kenny, "but the ball took a bad hop. I think it hit something."

"I know. I saw the way it bounced. Just remember to watch the ball all the way into your glove."

That's what the coach always said, and Jacob knew it was true. Maybe the coin had nothing to do with it.

At least things started looking better right away. Jonathan and Henry got solid hits off Hausberg, and Jenny brought Jonathan home with a line-drive single.

Jacob was coming up to bat. He told himself there was no jinx. Another hit and RBI

would reverse the damage, and he could forget about his bad play.

He dug in and readied himself, and he swung at the first pitch. He hit the ball hard on the ground toward the right side.

The first baseman dove. He stopped the ball, but he was stretched out on the grass. As he scrambled to his knees, big Hausberg was pounding his way toward first to cover the bag.

Jacob and House arrived together. Both feet slammed the bag, and the ball slapped into Hausberg's glove.

But Jacob was sure he had gotten there first. He had gone all out, and the luck had . . .

"*Yer out!!!*" the umpire called from across the infield.

Jacob spun around. "*What?*"

The umpire turned her back and walked away.

Jacob spun back toward his coach. "That's okay," Coach Wilkens said to him. "You moved the runners up. We'll bring them in."

"But I was *safe!*"

"I thought so too. But it was close."

All the Dodgers were yelling that Jacob had been robbed.

Jacob walked slowly back to the dugout. What a lousy break!

He felt even worse when Eddie and Billy failed to bring the runners home.

"Don't worry," Harlan told Jacob. "We're still up by three runs."

Harlan was getting his catching gear on. He was going into the game.

Kenny had no trouble with the bottom of the Giants' order. He did give up a two-out walk, but then he struck out the next batter.

The score was still 6 to 3 at the end of the fourth inning.

In the fifth the coach put Ben in at second base and put Anthony out in left field to replace Eddie.

Jacob talked to himself. "Keep your head in the game. Forget about that stupid coin," he kept saying.

He was sure that was the right way to think when he made a nice catch in the fifth on a pop-up to short right.

True, he grounded out in the bottom of

the fifth, but then Hausberg had settled down and was getting everyone out.

Jacob went into the sixth inning feeling pretty good about his game. But he was nervous. He didn't want to make another mistake.

Maybe Kenny was getting worried too. He walked the first batter and then got behind and grooved one to Hausberg.

The big guy clubbed a double down the left field line.

Then the catcher hit a bouncer that jumped over Jonathan's head and rolled into left field.

Two runs scored.

Suddenly the lead was cut to one, and the Giants hadn't made an out yet.

The Giants' fans were all standing and cheering, and their dugout was going crazy.

The little substitute center fielder was up next. Kenny took some long breaths and stepped to the rubber. He seemed to settle down. He struck out the rookie on three pitches.

That took some pressure off.

And then the other rookie, batting ninth,

rolled a grounder back to Kenny. Kenny made a good throw to first.

Two outs and a *lot* of pressure gone.

Now the Dodgers needed only one out.

But Nugent, the speedy lead-off hitter, was coming up.

Jacob watched Kenny's chest rise and fall a couple of times. Jacob was taking deep breaths too.

Kenny threw a hard fastball on the inside edge of the plate. The umpire called it a strike.

Kenny breathed again and so did Jacob. Then Kenny reared back and fired hard.

The pitch was a little outside, but Nugent reached for it and drove it into right field.

Jacob took off to his right. The ball was sinking fast and headed for the gap.

But Jacob was closing in on it.

Should he go for the ball or just make sure he got it on one hop? He could end the game if he could make the catch.

Suddenly he was diving.

But he shouldn't have.

The ball hit the grass in front of his glove and bounced on by.

Jacob jumped up and chased after it, but Sterling was coming hard. Jacob had to get out of Sterling's way, so he dropped to the grass, but his momentum carried him into Sterling's legs.

And Sterling went down.

Both boys scrambled up to get the ball. Sterling got there first, but by the time he could get a throw off, it was too late. Nugent had circled the bases.

Jacob couldn't believe it. This was his biggest mess-up, ever.

The Giants were ahead 7 to 6, and now the Dodgers only had one chance to turn that around.

When Kenny got the third out, the Dodgers all started yelling to each other that they could still win.

But Ben Riddle was coming up.

Jacob was sick. He sat at the end of the bench feeling like the biggest loser in the world.

Big Hausberg threw Ben curves, and Riddle struck out.

The big hitters were coming up, though, and Jacob let himself hope.

Kenny did his best. He hit a line drive. But it was straight at the third baseman. So now there were two outs.

Jonathan had had House's number all day, and maybe that worried the big guy. Suddenly he started having trouble throwing strikes. He walked Jonathan on four pitches.

The Dodgers were still alive . . . barely.

Then Sterling took an awkward swing and bounced an easy grounder to third base. Jacob dropped his head.

That meant the game was over and . . .

Then everyone on the bench cheered, and Jacob looked up. The third baseman had tried to go to second for the force, and he had thrown the ball into right field. The runners ended up on second and third, and Jenny was going to get a chance to win the game.

Jacob jumped up to watch, and then he realized he was on deck. He hurried out to get a bat.

But the Giants' coach had walked out to talk with the pitcher. And Jacob realized what was going to happen. The coach would rather put Jenny on first and make every

bag a force. And he probably thought Jacob was an easier out than Jenny.

He was probably right.

Jacob watched it all happen. The pitcher walked Jenny intentionally, and Jacob had to wait for the fourth pitch and then walk to the plate.

Everything was on the line for him.

He had lost the game, but now he could win it.

Or he could lose it twice.

He made up his mind to go down trying, and so he didn't stand there and hope for a walk.

He swung at the big curve and missed.

And then he swung and missed a fastball.

He was looking for the curve again. And he was right. This time he waited for it and hammered it hard.

The ball skipped in front of the shortstop and bounced off his chest. Jacob ran all out, hoping.

But the shortstop had time to chase the ball down and flip it to second for the force.

It was a close play, but Jacob watched the

umpire and saw her right arm fly up, and heard her yell, *"Out!"*

So that was that.

Jacob had lost the game, all by himself.

Or at least that's how he felt about it.

BOX SCORE, GAME 5

Blue Springs Giants				7		Angel Park Dodgers				6
	ab	r	h	rbi			ab	r	h	rbi
Nugent lf	4	1	1	2		Jie 2b	4	1	0	0
Sanchez ss	4	1	2	0		White 3b	3	0	1	1
Weight 3b	3	1	2	1		Sandoval p	4	1	2	0
Glenn 1b	3	0	1	1		Swingle ss	3	2	3	3
Cooper 2b	2	1	0	0		Malone cf	3	0	1	0
Hausberg p	3	1	1	0		Roper 1b	2	0	1	1
Dodero c	1	0	0	0		Scott rf	4	1	1	0
Villareal cf	1	1	1	0		Boschi lf	2	0	0	0
Spinner rf	1	0	0	0		Bacon c	2	1	1	1
Zonn c	2	1	1	2		Ruiz lf	1	0	0	0
Waganheim rf	2	0	0	0		Sloan c	1	0	1	0
Stevens cf	1	0	0	0		Riddle 3b	1	0	0	0
ttl	27	7	9	6			30	6	11	6

Giants   0 0 3   0 0 4—7
Dodgers 3 2 1   0 0 0—6

★ 6 ★

Hard Luck

The coach called everyone together, but Jacob slipped away. He didn't want to talk to the coach . . . or to his parents . . . or to his friends.

He just wanted to be alone.

So Jacob walked home by himself, and then he went to his backyard. He sat behind the garage and leaned against the wall. The day was hot as blazes, but Jacob didn't want to go inside and face . . . people.

He kept remembering: the two mistakes in right field; the close play at first; that final play that was so close.

Whether he called it bad luck or bad play, it all came down to the same thing. He had

been the one who lost the game. And yet, with just a little *good* luck, the whole thing could have been so different.

After a while Jacob's dad found him.

He came around the corner, as though he knew exactly where to look, and he said, "Are you okay, son?"

"Yup." Jacob really didn't want to hear one of his dad's pep talks right now.

"I hope you aren't taking that whole loss on your own shoulders."

"I'm not."

"That's what you say. But I can see how you look. Just remember, you hit that last ball hard. If it hadn't been right at the second baseman, you would have been the hero."

"Shortstop."

"What?"

"I hit it to the shortstop."

"I thought it was the kid out by second base."

"That's the shortstop. The second baseman is on the other side of second."

"Oh. Well, anyway, even Mom said it was almost a hit."

What he meant by "even Mom" was that

Jacob's mother knew a lot more about baseball than Dad did.

But Jacob only said, "I know, Dad."

Dad sat down next to him. He took his
glasses off and wiped the sweat from his eyes
with a white handkerchief. "I *do* understand how you feel. I remember a piano re-
cital one time when I messed up the whole
piece. By the time I was finished, I just
wanted to crawl out of the place."

"Is that what you think I did—mess
everything up?"

"Oh no. No. Not at all. You had a good
game. I'm just saying that I know how dis-
appointed you are."

Jacob didn't want to say it, but it was
hardly the same.

"Well, anyway," Dad finally said, "I guess
I'll leave you alone. I know you don't want
to talk. But, Jacob, I don't think you should
feel so bad about the way you played."

"I know."

Dad got up and left.

And Jacob tried to think why he did feel
so lousy. Mostly, everything seemed so un-
fair. Sometimes the ball bounced right, and
sometimes it didn't. But how come, on a day

like this, so many things had to go wrong?

Jacob stayed where he was for almost an hour, and then he got up and wandered into his house and sneaked upstairs to his room. But his mom heard him and came up. "Jacob," she said, "Kenny has called about three times in the last hour."

"Okay."

"Jacob?"

Oh, brother, another speech was coming. "Yeah?"

But Mom only said, "You played a good game. You don't need to be going around with your head down."

Mrs. Scott was a P.E. teacher and coach. She knew those things. But she didn't really understand what Jacob was feeling right now—not exactly.

"Anyway, call Kenny."

Jacob said, "Okay," but he didn't do it. He figured Kenny would call again.

Instead, Kenny showed up at the house. Mrs. Scott sent him up to Jacob's room.

"Hi, Jacob," he said as he came into the room.

Jacob was ready. "Kenny, I don't want to talk about the game. Okay?"

"Yeah, that's all right. I just wanted to tell you what you're doing wrong." Kenny smiled.

"What are you talking about, Kenny? Losing the game wasn't *my* fault."

"I know," Kenny said, and now he smiled wide, showing all those straight white teeth of his.

Jacob was still a little off guard. He had expected Kenny to tell him he had done all right. "I hit that last ball hard. I just—"

"I know all that, Jacob. You had lousy luck today."

"That's right."

"Jacob, my dad and I talked about all this stuff. He said that if you play long enough, *everything* happens—good and bad."

"What's that supposed to mean?"

"Well, for instance, on that last play, the shortstop got lucky when the ball bounced straight in front of him. But he did the right thing. He stayed in front of the ball. So he made some of his own luck."

Jacob was sitting on his bed. Kenny sat down on the floor, facing him. "Think about that ball you missed early in the game when you were charging in for it."

"It hit something and took a bad hop."

"I know. But you have to keep the ball in front of you, so if it does get under your glove, it hits you and doesn't get through. The same on that ball you dove for. The coach always says not to leave your feet unless you know for sure you can catch it—or someone is close enough to back you up."

Jacob remembered the coach telling him that. Still, if he had caught the ball, everyone would have carried him off the field on their shoulders.

"Kenny, a guy still needs some luck. I was just an inch or two from catching that ball. I could have won the game. Or what about that ball I hit at the end. If it had been a few feet to the left or right, we still would have won."

"I know. But you're really lunging at the ball, Jacob. You're dropping your shoulder and letting your head jump forward. That's why you topped the ball and hit it in the dirt. If you hold steady and stroke through the ball, you drive it."

Jacob didn't say anything for quite some time. He was thinking. Finally he said, "So you came over here to tell me that I wasn't

unlucky but that I *played bad*. Is that supposed to make me feel better?"

"Sure." Kenny grinned again. "You came home thinking you were jinxed. But you're not. That means you can change a few little things and have a great game next time."

Jacob couldn't help but smile. "I'd still feel better if I could find that stupid lucky coin," he said.

"Okay, let's take rakes and go over and look some more. But let's take bats, too, and I'll show you what I'm talking about with that swing of yours."

Jacob nodded, and he actually felt pretty good—better than he ever expected to feel.

But something was still bothering him. "Kenny, why do you think major-leaguers do all that stuff to get good luck?"

"I asked my dad about that," Kenny said. "He says luck *is* always part of the game. And everybody wishes they could find some way to control it. That's why they fool around with all that stuff—even though they know they just have to play the best they can."

Jacob figured that was probably right. But he still wished he had his coin back.

★ 7 ★

Inside Story

On Wednesday evening the Dodgers played the Mariners—a team they had beaten earlier that year.

Jacob and Kenny and Harlan walked to the game together. "Now that we've lost two games, we don't have much chance of catching the Giants for the first-half championship," Jacob told his friends.

"Maybe," Kenny told him. "But the Reds could still beat the Giants. And the Padres could too. We just have to win *our* games and then see what happens."

No matter how often Jacob tried to think about doing his best, some feeling kept hanging over him that he was jinxed. How

could his team ever win if that didn't change?

When the boys were about to cross the street to the park, Ben and Anthony came up behind them. "Hey, the benchwarmers should get a lot of playing time today," Harlan told them. "Let's hope the starters get some runs right away so we can get in early."

Ben shrugged. "I just mess up anyway," he said.

"Come on, Ben," Kenny said. "Don't say that. You're getting better every week."

"I still haven't had a hit," Ben said.

And Anthony added in his big, soft voice, "Me neither."

"Don't worry. You will," Harlan told them. "It took Jacob and me a while last year, but we finally started getting hits."

"I wish Jacob hadn't lost his lucky coin," Ben said.

The light changed, and the boys walked across the street. "Just concentrate on your *swing* and forget about luck," Kenny said.

"Hey, that thing gave me luck against the Padres," Anthony said. "I rubbed it and got

hit by a pitch, and then I scored the winning run."

"Good idea, Anthony," Kenny said.
"Maybe you can get your own lucky piece
and get hit by pitches all the time."

All the boys laughed. Even Jacob.

He told himself, again, not to worry about
luck.

But the game got off to a bad start. Eddie
Boschi was pitching for the Dodgers, and
he was having trouble with his control.

He walked the first two batters. Then he
finally made a good pitch and got a nice
ground ball that should have been an easy
out.

Kenny fielded it and decided to go to third
to force the lead runner. The throw was
perfect and in plenty of time.

But Henry dropped it.

It was in his glove, and then it simply fell
out.

Everyone was safe, and the bases were
loaded.

Jacob tried not to think about it. But it
seemed to him that bad luck was spreading
now. The major-league radio announcers

sometimes talked about how that could happen. A whole team could be "snake-bitten," and one bad thing after another would keep happening to them.

When the Mariners' big first baseman knocked home two runs with a bloop single, Jacob feared the worst.

Before the inning was over, Eddie walked two more batters, and one kid scored on a passed ball.

Four runs on one hit.

And that was a half-swing single.

Jacob trotted to the dugout. He could see that everyone looked worried.

"Come on, let's get those runs back," Jenny yelled, and everyone began shouting the same thing. But they didn't sound sure of themselves, the way they should be against the Mariners.

Lian struck out—something he almost never did. Henry got a single, and Kenny hit a long fly ball. But the center fielder had been playing very deep. He made a pretty good run, reached out his glove . . . and the ball dropped in.

No one was more surprised than the center fielder!

Jonathan hit a double and Henry scored, and then Sterling hit a high pop-up. The catcher staggered around awkwardly, but somehow he stayed with the ball and caught it.

"What is going on?" Jacob said to no one in particular, and then he grabbed his glove and headed back to right field.

How could they be behind the Mariners 4 to 1?

And then things got worse.

Eddie was really struggling. He started walking guys again. The Mariners scored two more runs in the second—again, on only one hit.

Jacob wondered how long the coach would stay with Eddie, but Coach Wilkens kept yelling to him to follow through and stop aiming the ball. And he kept clapping and yelling to the team, "Come on, kids, let's play some baseball."

Jacob was trying not to think it, but he felt doomed. Maybe nothing would ever go right again.

When he got back to the dugout, he sat down and tried to tell himself that everything was going to be all right. He rubbed

his sweaty hands on his pants and . . . felt something.

But it was too good to be true.

He pressed his fingers against the hard object inside his pant leg.

It was round, flat. It was . . . it was definitely . . .

"Hey, you guys, I found it!" he yelled. "My lucky coin. It's down inside my pants—in the lining."

"Let me rub it!" Ben said, and he came over to Jacob.

"I can't get it out without taking my pants off. Just rub it through my pant leg."

Ben smiled and gave it a good rub. "Thanks," he said. He suddenly looked a lot happier.

Jacob couldn't believe it. It had been there the whole time. It must have slipped through a hole in his pocket and into the lining.

"All right!" he yelled. "Now our luck changes! Everyone hits!" He laughed— mostly so the players wouldn't think he was all that serious—but inside, he really had a feeling things would change now.

Jacob didn't really get a big reaction from

the players. Most of them didn't seem to think it was that big of a deal.

But Anthony gave the coin a rub. "Now I *want* to play," he said.

Jenny paid no attention, but she smacked a line drive up the middle for a single.

Jacob started to hope.

Eddie's luck had been terrible all day; suddenly it changed too. He hit a ground ball that should have been an out, but the Mariner second baseman let it roll right between his legs.

"I told you! I told you!" Jacob yelled.

And then he started into his broadcast. "Hank, I believe this Dodger team has grabbed the momentum from the Mariners."

"That's exactly right, Frank. I think one of the Mariner kids was packing that momentum, and he must've dropped it—'cause those Dodgers pounced right on it."

The players started cheering, and Jacob could feel the change in the dugout. The Dodgers *were* starting to believe.

And Jacob was going out to the on-deck area. He was soon going to get a chance to make up for the last game.

When the Mariner pitcher walked Billy on four pitches, Jacob *knew* this was his great moment.

Bases loaded. What a perfect time to turn his luck around! He reached down and felt for the coin, and then he gave it a good rub.

"Knock it out of here!" Jonathan yelled to him.

Jacob nodded and stepped up to bat.

He could see that the pitcher had lost some of his early confidence. The first pitch was weak, and Jacob almost jumped off the ground, he swung so hard. He fouled the ball into the dirt.

"Be patient, Jacob," the coach yelled. "Make him pitch to you."

Jacob nodded and got set. The next pitch was outside and maybe a little low.

"*Steee-rike!*" the umpire called.

Jacob stepped back. He couldn't believe it. The ump was blind.

But that was okay. Luck was with him now.

He reached down and rubbed the coin and then stepped back in. He took a ball, low.

Then he got his pitch.

He strode into the pitch, swung hard . . .
And missed!
Completely.
Strike three!

★ 8 ★

Time to Play

Jacob walked back to the dugout. At the last second he remembered he still had the bat in his hand. He sort of flipped it in the direction of the bat rack, and then he walked in and plunked himself down on the bench.

How could this happen to him?

"Jacob, you're still lunging at the ball."

Jacob looked up to see Kenny standing over him. "What?"

"Forget about that stupid lucky coin and think about your swing. Your shoulder and head are dropping. You're swinging over the ball."

But Jacob couldn't even think about that stuff right now.

"Sometimes luck doesn't change all at once," he told Kenny. "Sometimes you have to come out of a slump a little at a time."

But just then all the players jumped to their feet. Lian had whacked a line drive into right field.

Jenny and Eddie scored, and Billy hustled into third.

"All right!" Jonathan was yelling. "Now we turn this thing around. Get us some more runs, Henry."

Kenny had to go get a bat. He was on deck. "Anyway, think about keeping your head and shoulders steady," he told Jacob as he walked away.

Henry took a pitch inside, and the Dodgers all yelled, "Good eye, Henry! Make him pitch to you."

Henry did just that, and he ended up walking.

The bases were loaded again.

And then Kenny took that sweet stroke of his and roped a drive into left center. When the center fielder misplayed it and let it roll to the fence, three runs scored and Kenny ended up on third.

Then Jonathan hit a zinger of a single, and the Dodgers were on top.

Sterling kept the rally going with a pop-fly single of his own, and then Jenny picked up another walk to load the bases all over again.

Jacob was feeling better. Things had turned around. The luck was on their side now, and next time up he would get in on it. He might even get up again this inning the way things were going.

It didn't happen, though. Eddie swung hard and only ticked the ball. It dropped in front of the plate. The catcher grabbed it and touched home plate ahead of Jonathan, who was dashing in from third.

Then Billy bounced out, and the rally was over. But the Dodgers were ahead, 7 to 6, and they were rolling.

Jacob hustled out to right field. He would be leading off in the next inning, and he couldn't wait.

But one thing hadn't changed. Eddie couldn't seem to get the ball over the plate. He walked the first batter, got a fly-ball out, and then walked another kid.

Jacob yelled to him, "Come on, Eddie, throw strikes. We'll back you up."

But he was really wondering why the coach didn't bring Jonathan in to take Eddie's place.

And then the batter—the fast center fielder—cracked a hard shot straight at Jacob. Jacob started forward and then realized that the ball was really carrying. He took a few quick steps back and jumped, but the ball whizzed over his glove.

Jacob chased it down and threw hard and strong, keeping the runner to a double, but two runs scored and the Mariners were ahead again, 8 to 7.

Jacob tried to talk to himself. The guy had really tagged the ball. He just misjudged it for a second. That didn't prove that he was still jinxed.

At that point the coach walked out and had a talk with Eddie. And Eddie did seem to do something different. He got big Rodriguez to pop up in foul territory, and then he struck out the good-hitting third baseman.

Jacob jogged in and found his bat. He

gave his lucky coin a good rub. This was it. His luck was going to change.

He didn't worry about practice swings; he just pictured himself blasting that ball somewhere and getting the inning started right.

He stepped up to the plate, got a good pitch . . . and topped the ball.

He hit a slow roller to the first baseman.

He just couldn't figure out what was going on.

Lian also grounded out. Then Henry singled and so did Kenny. But Jonathan hit a ground ball to the third baseman. The kid stepped on third, and that was the inning. The Mariners were still ahead.

At least Eddie got the Mariners out—one, two, three—in the top of the fourth.

And Sterling started things off in the bottom of the inning with a booming double.

Jacob sat on the bench, gripping his lucky coin through the fabric of his pants. He tried to feel the luck flowing right into his fingers. "Bring Sterling home!" he yelled to Jenny.

But then Kenny sat down by him. "Jacob,

listen to me," he said. "Get rid of that stupid lucky charm, and think about what you're doing at the plate."

Jacob let go of the coin and said, "I *am* thinking about it."

Kenny was really serious now. "Remember that game against the Padres, when you went 3 for 3? What were you doing different? And don't tell me you were having good luck."

"I don't know. I just—"

"Well, I'll tell you. You were keeping your head still and your shoulders level, the way the coach always says to do. You weren't jumping at the ball."

Jacob thought about that.

But he was watching Jenny too. He saw how steady she held her head and shoulders—just the way Kenny said—and then he saw her smooth stride, with her shoulders level, and her clean, even swing.

And he saw the ball *shoot* into right field!

She had banged out another hit, and suddenly the Dodgers were tied.

Jacob wondered. Wasn't the momentum coming back to them again? Wasn't that luck?

But Kenny didn't think so. "If you want to hit, swing the bat the way Jenny does," he said. "The luck is in your *batting stroke,* not in that stupid—"

"Stroke of luck," Jacob mumbled to himself, and he smiled. It really did make sense.

Then Eddie took a nice stroke himself, and he knocked out a nice single. Jacob was on deck again, and the Dodgers were starting to come alive again.

The Mariners' pitcher seemed to see what was happening too, and he lost a little of his cool. He walked Harlan, who was now batting in Billy's place.

Jacob was coming up with the bases loaded once again.

He rubbed his leg, just enough to get a touch of the lucky piece. Maybe Kenny was right, but . . .

"No, think about your stroke," he told himself.

The first pitch came in, fat as a balloon, and Jacob took a big cut.

And missed.

"Jacob, keep your head still. Don't lunge."

It was the coach, saying the same thing Kenny had said.

Jacob stepped out of the box and thought it all through. He concentrated this time. He knew he had to do it.

The pitch was outside. Jacob started to swing and held up.

"That was better," Kenny yelled. "You took a good stride. Now watch the ball all the way in and meet it."

And this time Jacob did it!

The ball was over the plate, and he followed it all the way in. He took a smooth swing and *met* the ball.

And he hit it *on the nose!*

The ball jumped off his bat!

It shot down the line in left and carried on the fly all the way to the fence. Jacob blasted around first and then saw that he could trot over to second with a stand-up double.

Two runs scored, and the Dodgers were on top again.

"Hey, Jacob," Kenny yelled. "Now that's what I call a stroke of luck!"

Jacob grinned and shook his fists, and then he yelled to Lian to keep the inning going.

Lian did. He took his own good swing and

knocked the ball into center field. Two more runs scored, and the rout was on.

Before the inning was over, six runs had crossed the plate and the Dodgers were ahead 13 to 8.

And before the game was over, Jacob had gotten another hit and driven in another run.

The Dodgers kept rolling after that, and the final score was 18 to 8. But the best thing of all was what happened to Ben Riddle. When the coach put him in the game, he asked Jacob for a rub of his lucky coin.

Jacob let him rub it, but then he talked to him about his swing. "Swing like you're reaching for the ball with your hands," he told him. "Stride, but don't jerk or bend— just step forward and take a smooth swing."

And Ben did it.

Ben poked the ball straight up the middle and drove in a run. And then he came around to score.

With a grin as wide as his face!

Anthony didn't get a hit, but he made the final put-out of the game when he caught a fly ball in center field.

So he was happy.

And Jacob was feeling *GREAT*.

Eddie had gotten through a tough day, and with the coach's help, ended up pitching well in the late innings. So he was happy too.

The whole team was feeling a lot better.

Kenny got hold of Jacob once all the celebrating was over. "See. See," he said. "Now you're swinging the bat the way you should. That's what the trouble was."

"Yeah, my lucky coin finally came through," Jacob said, and he grinned.

Kenny shook his head and laughed.

"Well, all I can say is, you better keep that good stroke. We've gotta win all our games if we're gonna win the first-half championship."

Jacob agreed, but he asked his friends to stand in front of him while he unbuttoned his pants long enough to reach in and pull the coin out of the lining. Maybe the coin didn't make any difference—but he didn't want to lose it again.

"There's my sweet little partner," Jacob said as he pulled the coin out. "I never could have . . . hey, wait a minute! This isn't even

it. This is the lucky charm I got out of a cereal box last year—and it never did work very well."

Kenny and Harlan laughed hard.

And then so did Jacob. "Oh, well. I guess if you wait long enough, a good-luck charm will finally start working," he said.

"Especially if you swing the bat right," Kenny told him.

"Yeah, that too."

Kenny and Harlan shook their heads and laughed. And then Jacob did the last thing they expected. He flipped the good-luck charm in a garbage can.

"Don't you believe in good-luck charms anymore?" Harlan asked him.

"Nah. That was stupid."

"Now you're talking," Kenny said.

But Jacob's gap-toothed grin appeared again. "I think it was this new pair of socks that turned my luck around," he said.

"Oh, brother!" Kenny said, but all three boys were laughing.

But Jacob knew exactly what he had to do from now on. "Well, Hank, Jacob Scott caught fire today," he said in his announc-

er's voice. "He's got a sweet swing when he concentrates on the fundamentals."

"Yeah, I'd say so, Frank. The boy has it going now. I think he's about to take over as the star of this team."

"Yes, and if he can teach Sandoval and Sloan to swing the bat the way he does, they should do well too."

"Oh, brother!" Kenny and Harlan both said.

And Jacob grinned. All the way home.

BOX SCORE, GAME 6

San Lorenzo Mariners 8

	ab	r	h	rbi
Cisco lf	2	2	1	0
Smagler 2b	2	2	0	0
Cast cf	2	2	1	2
Rodriguez 1b	3	1	2	3
Sullivan 3b	4	0	1	0
Klein rf	1	0	0	0
Bernhardt ss	2	0	0	2
Gilbert p	3	0	0	0
Korman c	2	1	0	0
Watson p	1	0	0	0
Casper 1b	1	0	0	0
Rondeau rf	1	0	1	0
ttl	**24**	**8**	**6**	**7**

Angel Park Dodgers 18

	ab	r	h	rbi
Jie 2b	4	2	2	3
White 3b	4	2	2	0
Sandoval ss	5	2	4	5
Swingle lf	5	0	4	5
Malone cf	4	1	2	0
Roper 1b	4	2	2	1
Boschi p	3	3	2	0
Bacon c	1	1	0	0
Scott rf	4	2	2	3
Sloan c	1	2	1	0
Riddle 2b	1	1	1	1
Ruiz lf	1	0	0	0
	37	**18**	**22**	**18**

Mariners 4 2 2 0 0 0—8
Dodgers 1 6 0 6 5 x—18

Second Season

League standings after six games:

Giants	6–0
Dodgers	4–2
Reds	3–3
Padres	3–3
Mariners	1–5
A's	0–6

Fourth game scores:

Dodgers	4	Padres	3
Mariners	4	Reds	3
Giants	17	A's	0

Fifth game scores:

Giants	7	Dodgers	6
Padres	8	Reds	2
Mariners	3	A's	1

Sixth game scores:

Dodgers	18	Mariners	8
Reds	7	A's	4
Giants	3	Padres	2

JONATHAN SWINGLE

At-bats	Runs	Hits	RBIs	Avg.
18	4	12	11	.667

KENNY SANDOVAL

At-bats	Runs	Hits	RBIs	Avg.
20	7	10	9	.500

JACOB SCOTT

At-bats	Runs	Hits	RBIs	Avg.
18	6	9	8	.500

SECOND-YEAR STATISTICS

JENNY ROPER

At-bats	Runs	Hits	RBIs	Avg.
18	5	9	6	.500

SECOND-YEAR STATISTICS

LIAN JIE

At-bats	Runs	Hits	RBIs	Avg.
20	5	9	5	.450

SECOND-YEAR STATISTICS

HARLAN SLOAN

At-bats	Runs	Hits	RBIs	Avg.
7	3	3	1	.429

SECOND-YEAR STATISTICS

HENRY WHITE

At-bats	Runs	Hits	RBIs	Avg.
21	7	9	1	.420

STERLING MALONE

At-bats	Runs	Hits	RBIs	Avg.
17	4	6	3	.352

SECOND-YEAR STATISTICS

EDDIE BOSCHI

At-bats	Runs	Hits	RBIs	Avg.
15	5	5	1	.333

BILLY BACON

At-bats	Runs	Hits	RBIs	Avg.
8	4	2	3	.250

BEN RIDDLE

At-bats	Runs	Hits	RBIs	Avg.
8	1	1	1	.125

ANTHONY RUIZ

At-bats	Runs	Hits	RBIs	Avg.
7	1	0	0	.000

ALL-STAR OF THE MONTH

JENNY ROPER

Jenny Roper is a natural. She's not only one of the best players on the Angel Park Dodgers, she's also one of the stars of the entire league. She's a great hitter and a steady fielder, and she is very fast. On top

of that, she gets along well with everyone, and she fires up the team with her timely hitting and her good attitude.

When Jenny was in third grade, she was one of the best athletes in the school. She went out for the mostly boys' Little League team—and she made it. She had been playing sports with her two big brothers all her life, so competing with boys didn't bother her a bit.

By the time she was in her fifth-grade season, she was voted to the league's all-star team. And no wonder! She batted .477 and was one of the best clutch hitters in the league. And no one played first base with fewer errors. She was known for her sure fielding as well as her ability to dig hard throws out of the dirt.

And if that wasn't enough, she started her sixth-grade season *blazing* hot. In her first six games she batted a whopping .500 and drove in six runs! At the same time she was teaching younger players to get ready to take over for her at first once she finished this, her last season. She is not the player on the

team who is most likely to hit a home run, but with runners on base, or in a tight situation, Jenny is the one the Dodgers like to have coming up to bat.

When Jenny was younger, she took a lot of teasing from the boys on other teams. She hated that, and it bothered her. Now that she plays so well, she can shut up most guys with her bat, but she still resents it when people talk about her being "good for a girl." As she has grown older, she has become more aware that some people think girls should not play sports with boys, but she tries not to let that upset her.

Jenny has many interests. She's good at all sports, but she is especially interested in golf. She thinks she may like to pursue a career as a professional. She also has interests outside sports. She's a good artist, and she takes piano lessons. She has lots of girlfriends, and she likes to spend time with them, between all her practices. She's not one to spend a lot of days hanging out at the local mall, or going to movies, but she admits that she probably wastes too much

time talking on the phone. Fortunately, she's a very good student and seems to keep up without having to work all that hard—and that gives her time to do the many things she likes to do.

Lately Jenny has started to notice boys. When she's on the baseball diamond, she just thinks of herself as another athlete, and the fact that the other players are boys doesn't matter. But a couple of junior high boys have really caught her attention. One of them has been calling a lot lately. Baseball, you might say, has not been the only thing on her mind.

DEAN HUGHES has written many books for children, including the popular *Nutty* stories and *Jelly's Circus*. He has also published such works of literary fiction for young adults as the highly acclaimed *Family Pose*. Writing keeps Mr. Hughes very busy, but he does find time to run and play golf—and he loves to watch almost all sports. His home is in Utah. He and his wife have three children, all in college.

◀ **READ THESE OTHER ANGEL**

"A thoroughly enjoyable series."
—*Publishers Weekly*

#1 MAKING THE TEAM

Kenny, Harlan, and Jacob have officially made the team, but some of the older players—mostly team bully Rodney Bunson—seem bent on making life miserable for the three rookies. Can the third-grade Little Leaguers stand up to some big-league bullying?

#2 BIG BASE HIT

Awkward and big for his age, Harlan seems to do everything wrong—and it's making him wonder whether he really belongs on the team at all. But then the pitcher throws the ball, and Harlan gives the team just what they've all been waiting for: a big base hit!

#3 WINNING STREAK

Kenny's in a slump—and it spells big trouble for the undefeated Angel Park Dodgers. Jacob's got a few tricks that he thinks will help, but his wacky ideas only seem to make matters worse. Then he hits on the one trick that puts Kenny back in action, just in time to put the team back on a winning streak!

#4 WHAT A CATCH!

Brian desperately wants to make his last season in Little League his best ever, but his mistakes might cost the team the championship. The All-Stars try to help their nervous friend build his self-confidence, but it takes a pep talk from a major-league pro to get Brian back on track.

PARK ALL-STARS BY DEAN HUGHES

#5 ROOKIE STAR

Does Kenny think he's too good for his old friends?
He's been seen practicing with some older players,
and the local paper runs an article calling him a
"rookie star." Jacob and Harlan think he's got a bad
case of swollen head, and the whole team starts
fighting. Can they get it together before it's too late?

#6 PRESSURE PLAY

Their rivals are playing dirty and the Dodgers are
starting to lose their spirit as well as their tempers.
Jacob, benched because of slipping grades, sees that
it's up to him to use his brains instead of his bat to
come up with a solution that will put the Dodgers
back in the running for the championship. But how?

#7 LINE DRIVE

When the Dodgers' second baseman breaks his leg,
no one expects that Coach Wilkens will choose little
Lian Jie, a new player from the minor league, to take
his place. Harlan can see that Lian Jie's got the right
stuff to be a Dodger, but how can he help the new
kid prove it to the rest of the team?

#8 CHAMPIONSHIP GAME

The Dodgers have a shot at the league title, but
they're puzzled by Coach Wilkens's strange behavior.
First he takes star slugger Rodney Bunson out of the
game, and then he starts coaching players on other
teams. Can the Dodgers keep their coach from
wrecking their chances at the championship?

BULLSEYE BOOKS PUBLISHED BY ALFRED A. KNOPF, INC.

How could his own parents be so cruel?

The Kid in the Red Jacket

by Barbara Park

Howard can't believe it. First, his parents decide to move the family halfway across the country, forcing him to leave all his friends behind. Then, they buy a house on a street called Chester Pewe—how embarrassing! Now, to top it all off, they expect him to be nice to the pesky six-year-old who lives in the house next door. How do they expect him to make any real friends with *her* tagging along behind him? At the rate things are going, Howard could spend the rest of his life known only by the color of his sportswear!

"A laugh-filled junior novel...Shrewdly drawn characters carry the day." —*Booklist*

"Funny, but full of real-life situations deftly handled."
—*Philadelphia Inquirer*

A *Parents' Choice* "Gold" Award Winner
An IRA-CBC Children's Choice

BULLSEYE BOOKS PUBLISHED BY ALFRED A. KNOPF

Women's work—ugh!

Justin and the Best Biscuits in the World

by Mildred Pitts Walter

Justin is sick of being the only male in the house. His mother and his sisters are always bossing him around—making him do "women's work," like washing dishes, cleaning his room, and making his bed. So naturally Justin is excited when his cowboy grandfather invites him to his ranch. He'll get to see the big rodeo, mend fences, catch fish, and do "men's work." But what Justin doesn't realize is that all kinds of work are important—including learning how to make the best biscuits in the world!

"Refreshing, likeable characters, an exciting rodeo and a history of the black cowboys combine to create a very special story." —*Publishers Weekly*

BULLSEYE BOOKS PUBLISHED BY ALFRED A. KNOPF, INC.

*Julian's small, but he sure can tell some tall tales
in these two award-winning books by Ann Cameron
with pictures by Ann Strugnell!*

The Stories Julian Tells

Julian, that quick fibber and wishful thinker, is great at telling
stories. He can make people—especially Huey, his younger
brother—believe just about anything. But some stories can
get you into a pack of trouble, and that's exactly where Julian
and Huey find themselves all too often!

An ALA Notable Children's Book
Winner of the Irma Simonton Black Award

More Stories Julian Tells

Even though Julian is a little older now, he still has plenty of
great stories left in him. Like the one about the time his best
friend Gloria proved she really did have the power to move
the sun and (finally!) won a bet with Julian. Sometimes,
though, Julian's way with words can backfire. How come he
gets into so much trouble when he hates trouble so much?

An ALA Notable Children's Book
A *School Library Journal* Best Book of the Year

BULLSEYE BOOKS PUBLISHED BY ALFRED A. KNOPF, INC.

D0290313